W9-BUB-285

DISNEY

VILLAINS

QUEEN OF HEARTS

Written by
Steve Behling
Illustrated by the
Disney Storybook Art Team

Greetings, loyal subjects!
I am the Queen of Hearts.
I rule all of Wonderland.
Welcome to MY book about ME!

Being QUEEN is hard work.

That is why I sleep all night.

A queen needs her beauty rest!

When I wake up, I must get ready
to greet my subjects.
Now where did I put that crown?

While I am getting ready,
my card soldiers train.
I make them run through
a maze every morning.
Why? Because I can. That is why!

Do you like PARADES? So do I!
That is why I have a parade
each and EVERY morning.

RED is my favorite color.

I love red so much.

I want to see it EVERYWHERE!

If something is not red, my cards
PAINT it red!
My cards are good painters . . .
or else it is off with their heads!

After a busy morning,
I like to have a SNACK.
Sometimes the White Rabbit
brings me berries to eat.

Sometimes the berries are
so YUMMY in my tummy
I could eat them all day long!

But other times, the berries are
NOT so yummy.
Then I become angry!
When this happens,
the White Rabbit runs away.

The White Rabbit comes back.

He brings me a cupcake.

First I am happy.

But when I try to take a bite . . .

it is NOT a cupcake after all!

Now it is off with his head.

"Off with his head!" I yell.

Lucky for the White Rabbit,

I do not stay mad for long.

After all, I am a kind queen.

After my snack,
I like to get some exercise.
A good game of croquet is just
the thing . . . if only those cards
would stay still!

I like to play
against the White Rabbit.
He tries to win the game.
But he will NEVER beat me.
Because I am the QUEEN!

Ask almost anyone,
and they will tell you.
I am the BEST croquet player
in Wonderland!

But the Cheshire Cat does not agree.
HE thinks he can make me lose
with his tricks.
But he is WRONG!

Oh, that cat makes me so MAD!
Why, I could just scream.
You know, I think I WILL!
"Off with his head!"
That is what I like to say.
"Off with his head!"
I could say that ALL day!

Oh, no! Would you look at the time?
It is late afternoon already!
That means it is TRIAL TIME!
I like to hold three trials every day.
It keeps everyone on their toes!

Trials are so much FUN!
I get to say,
"Off with their heads!"
I wish I got to say that
more often.
Oh, well.
We cannot have
everything we want.
Well, except for me.
I AM the queen, after all!

It has been a VERY long day.
There were so many games,
treats, and trials.
I must get some sleep!
But what is that?

I hear STRANGE sounds.

They keep me awake.

I get out of bed.

What could they be?

Oh, how silly of me!
It is only the creaking of my
heart-shaped rocking chair.

I do so love hearts, you know.
They make me so HAPPY!

In fact, they make me SO happy
I scream, "Off with their heads!"
It is a perfect end to a perfect day.
At last I am ready to sleep.
Oh, it is GOOD to be the queen!